I didn't see the kids until they'd stepped from the dark corner right into my pathway.

"Hey, kid, whatcha doin'?" taunted the taller one.

"Lemme see that," said the other one, as he grabbed for my backpack.

My heart was pounding so hard I thought my chest was going to pop open. I just stood there like a dummy, not saying a word.

It was hard to tell how old the boys were, but in the dark tunnel, they seemed like giants.

"I said, lemme see that." The second guy made another grab at my pack.

"Ya got any money?" His voice sounded like a gangster in a TV movie—only I couldn't turn the channel and make him go away. Was this really happening? In the movies, this was when the hero leaped into action, but my feet felt like they were super-glued to the ground. . . .

Ask for these titles from Chariot Books:
Project Cockroach
The Best Defense
Adam Straight to the Rescue
Adam Straight and the Mysterious Neighbor
Mystery on Mirror Mountain
Courage on Mirror Mountain

A JOSH McINTIRE BOOK

THE BEST

Defense

Elaine K. McEwan

Chariot Books™
David C. Cook Publishing Co.

To Patrick

Chariot Books™ is an imprint of David C. Cook Publishing Co.
David C. Cook Publishing Co., Elgin, Illinois 60120
David C. Cook Publishing Co., Weston, Ontario
Nova Distribution, Ltd., Torquay, England

Cover design by Elizabeth Thompson
Cover illustration by Mel Williges
First printing, 1991
Printed in the United States of America
95 94 93 92   5 4 3 2

Library of Congress Cataloging-in-Publication Data
McEwan, Elaine K.
    The Best Defense: a Josh McIntire Book/ by Elaine K.
McEwan
        p. cm.
    Summary: Fifth grader Josh McIntire learns to deal with his
problems by means of karate and prayer.
ISBN 1-55513-358-4
[1. Christian life—Fiction.] I. Title.
PZ7.M4784545Be 1991
[Fic]—dc20   91-11221
                                              CIP
                                              AC

I watched the water inch slowly to the top of the toilet bowl. Another minute and it was going to overflow. Nothing worked very well in this crummy house. I wished we were back with my dad in Woodview. But I didn't have time to daydream—the water was really pouring out now. I threw some towels on the floor to soak up the puddles and wondered what to do next.

I could call my mom at work, but she'd only been there a couple of months, and I didn't want to get her in trouble. I could call my dad, but I didn't have his phone number. Or I could call Wendell.

Wendell Hathaway lives next door, but I'm ambivalent about him. I just learned that word last week. If you're ambivalent about something, you can't decide whether you're crazy about it or you hate it. And that's the way I feel about Wendell. Sometimes I think he's the most terrific person in the whole world, like the time he called the paramedics when I broke my leg. Other times, he just drives me crazy . . . like when he wears weird clothes. If they published a list of the ten worst-dressed fifth graders in the world, Wendell would be number one.

But with the water on our bathroom floor getting deeper every minute, this was no time for ambivalence.

"Wendell," I pleaded into the telephone, "can you come right over? My toilet's overflowing."

By the time Wendell reached the back door, the trickle had turned into a torrent. I squished across the kitchen floor, my wet gym shoes leaving muddy footprints. I skidded to a stop and let him in.

I was really glad to see him even if he was wearing one of his most disgusting outfits. But we didn't have time to talk fashion. Clothes don't seem that important when you're drowning in toilet water.

We sloshed across the kitchen floor and peered into the bathroom. The water was still bubbling up over the rim of the toilet. The towels I'd thrown on the floor were sopping wet. Wendell reached over and turned a small faucet underneath the toilet. The water immediately stopped running.

I felt like a real jerk. "How'd you know to do that?" I asked.

"My dad showed me once," he answered.

Suddenly I felt sick to my stomach. I didn't have a dad around to show me how to fix toilets.

When my mom got home from work, Wendell and I were on our knees mopping up the kitchen floor. Mom looked like she didn't know whether to laugh or cry.

"What happened?" she asked.

I told her about the toilet, and Wendell showed her what he'd done.

"What do we do now?" Her question didn't seem to be addressed to either of us, and she had tears in her eyes. I wished I could help, but I didn't have a clue.

Once again, Wendell came to the rescue. "Why don't you call the landlord?" he suggested.

Mom smiled and patted him on the shoulder. "What would we do without you, Wendell?"

That made me feel a little jealous. After all, I was supposed to be the "man of the house." Weird Wendell was taking over my job.

The landlord called a handyman and before we knew it, our plumbing problems were history. But it was almost bedtime, and I'd totally forgotten about my homework assignment for Tuesday.

"Mom, you've got to tell me all about my ancestors. I need to know for school."

She didn't look thrilled. Her job as an executive secretary kept her busy all day long, and she was tired. "I don't think I have the energy to talk about ancestors tonight, Joshua. Can't it wait?"

"That's okay, Mom," I said. "I'll tell Mrs. Bannister I don't have any ancestors."

Actually Mrs. Bannister probably wouldn't have a hard time believing that. After my classmate Ben Anderson and I dumped a truckload of cockroaches in her desk drawer at the beginning of the school year, it was a miracle that she still spoke to me.

"We can talk at breakfast," Mom said.

"I'll figure it out," I said. "Maybe Dad will call, and I can ask about his relatives."

"Don't count on it, Joshua," she said with a wistful look. "I'm not sure we can depend on your father for anything right now."

Wendell rang my doorbell promptly at 8:15 the next morning. "How's your toilet feeling this morning?" he asked. "Has it stopped throwing up?"

I groaned inside. I sure hoped Wendell wasn't going to talk about my plumbing problems at school.

"My toilet's fine," I muttered. "Did you get your ancestor assignment done?"

"Yeah. I found out some really great stuff about my grandfather. He died before I was born, but he was in the CIA."

"The Central Intelligence Agency?" I asked, impressed.

"Yeah. The ones who spy on foreign countries."

8

I didn't have anything interesting to report. In fact, I hadn't done the assignment. I'd fallen asleep wondering what my dad was doing and why he didn't call more often.

When we got to school, Wendell went inside to help the computer teacher figure out how to play a new game. He knew more about computers than she did. I was glad to see him and his weird outfit disappear through the double doors. Was the guy color blind or trying to start a new fashion trend?

I headed round the corner and up the hill.

Ben Anderson called to me from across the playground. "Hey, Josh, wanna shoot some hoops?"

Since the cockroach caper and a disastrous outing to the railroad tracks (that ended up with my leg in a cast), I was uneasy about anything that involved Ben, even if it appeared to be a harmless game of basketball. But he was popular, and I didn't want him to think I was holding a grudge, so I joined the game.

Jefferson School is old, but we've got two new basketball hoops and smooth blacktop. Sometimes Mr. Shonkwiler, a sixth-grade teacher, plays with us. He's pretty good, but not as good as Mrs. Ravenswood, who teaches fourth grade. She played basketball in college. One day at recess she hit twenty straight free throws.

The bell rang, and we all ran to line up. Ben was right behind me.

"What are you gonna be for the Jefferson Masquerade?" he asked.

"The which?" I said, looking blank.

"It's a big deal. Every fall everybody dresses up, even the teachers, for a big parade. The Student Council gives prizes for the best costumes."

"What are you gonna be?"

"I can't tell you. It's a surprise."

I could tell Ben was planning to win, but maybe I could give him some competition. I love costumes. Once I wrapped myself in strips of old sheets to be a mummy. Another time I turned myself into a table. I looked pretty funny with my head sticking through a big cardboard box. I'd pasted paper plates and cups on top of an old checkered tablecloth on top.

But I had more pressing problems than a costume for a school parade. Mrs. Bannister was calling for our ancestor assignments, and all I had was a blank page. I slipped it in under the rest of the papers from my row and passed it forward.

"Use the next ten minutes to write in your journals, class," Mrs. Bannister said. "I want to look through your ancestor assignments."

Now I've had it, I thought. I took my journal notebook out of my desk and tried to act busy in case Mrs. Bannister looked my way. I started to write out all of the reasons I didn't have my assignment done, just in case she asked.

10

There are two main reasons I don't have my ancestor assignment done for today. The first reason is because of my plumbing problems.

I thought for a minute. Did I really want Mrs. Bannister to know about my leaky toilet? Well, why not? She might feel sorry for me and let me off the hook. Mrs. Bannister is pretty tough when it comes to homework assignments. If they aren't done, you stay in from recess to finish them or get a detention. But there was no harm in trying. . . .

My toilet overflowed last night, and by the time we called for a plumber and mopped all the water up and ate dinner, my mother was too tired to talk about ancestors. The second reason is my dad.

This was going to be a little harder to talk about. Sometime when I think about my dad I get all choked up and get tears in my eyes. I certainly didn't want to cry in front of Mrs. Bannister. I glanced up. She was busy grading papers.

I needed to talk to my dad about the ancestors, and I don't know where he is or how to reach him.

Writing about this was a real mistake. I was feeling crummier by the minute.

"Joshua."

Mrs. Bannister's voice startled me. I jumped and made a funny grunting noise, and everybody laughed.

"Could I see you for a minute, please?"

My face turned a bright red as I made my way to her desk. Mrs. Bannister and I had been getting along pretty well lately. She was fair and told interesting stories about her cats.

She whispered quietly in my ear, "Why didn't you do your ancestor assignment, Joshua? You turned in a blank page." She held it up, looking puzzled and disappointed.

My mind felt as blank as the page.

"Joshua? Let's talk about this at recess. Maybe by then you'll have an answer."

I went back to my seat. Wendell looked questioningly at me as I glanced in his direction. Ben snickered behind his hand. Everyone else was quietly writing.

After journal writing, Mrs. Bannister discussed the ancestor assignment. We were going to build a family tree, she explained, and write in the names of our grandparents and great-grandparents and where they came from. Then we were going to write our autobiographies—that's the story of somebody's life that the person writes himself. We could include pictures of ourselves when we were younger, and even write about what we wanted to be when we grew up. It didn't sound too bad.

When the bell rang, the class was out of the room like a shot. We were supposed to walk quietly in the halls, but everyone seemed to have forgotten the rules today. Instead of marching out to remind everyone the way she usually did, Mrs. Bannister stayed at her desk and motioned me forward.

I looked down at my Nike gym shoes. They were a little scuffed, but they still made me feel good. They gave me the courage to keep walking.

"Joshua, I didn't want to embarrass you in front of the class," Mrs. Bannister began, "but do you have an explanation for this blank page?"

I decided to be honest. I told her about the toilet and my dad. The words tumbled out of my mouth, and Mrs. Bannister listened quietly. Then she just folded the blank paper in half and handed it to me.

"Do you think you can work this out tonight, Joshua?" she asked.

"Oh, yes, Mrs. Bannister, I'll get it all done tonight. Really, I promise—"

She interrupted my babbling.

"Why don't you go out for recess now, Joshua? I'm going to the teachers' lounge to get a cup of coffee. I think we both deserve a break, don't you?"

Her comment surprised me. She was talking to me like I was a real person and not just a kid. I smiled and nodded.

"Thanks, Mrs. Bannister."

I ran out into the hallway, whistling as I went. Mrs. Bannister didn't even remind me to be quiet.

When the bell rang, I shoved my homework into my backpack and took off. I didn't feel like talking to anyone, but heading home to an empty house didn't sound good either. I hadn't been by Studebaker's Leather Emporium for a long time, and I wondered if the white leather coat I'd admired in September was still in the window.

The tunnel beneath the commuter railroad tracks was a good shortcut, and its cool darkness felt refreshing. I was so preoccupied thinking about my ancestors and my costume for the Jefferson Masquerade that I didn't see the kids until they'd stepped right into my pathway.

"Hey, kid. Whatcha doin'?" taunted the taller one.

"Lemme see that," said the other one, as he grabbed for my backpack.

My heart was pounding so hard I thought my chest was going to pop open. I just stood there like a dummy, not saying a word.

It was hard to tell how old the boys were, but in the dark tunnel, they seemed like giants. Giants in jeans and black leather jackets.

"I said, lemme see that." The second guy wasn't that tall, but his mean, pimply face was scary looking. He made another grab at my pack.

"Ya got any money?" His voice sounded like a gangster in a TV movie—only I couldn't turn the channel and make him go away. Was this really happening? In the movies, this was when the hero leaped into action, but my feet felt like they were super-glued to the ground.

"This kid is making me mad," said the pimply-faced attacker. "Don't he know how to talk?"

"I d-d-don't have any money," I stuttered. At least my voice had come back.

They grabbed my pack and began rummaging through it, tossing books and papers onto the ground. Just then we heard voices.

"Let's get outta here. He ain't got no money."

Obviously he hadn't had Mrs. Bannister for fifth grade. She wouldn't have put up with his grammar. They darted out the side exit and up the stairs.

The voices got closer, and I could see a bunch of little girls laughing and talking. I began to pick up my stuff out of the slimy gook that coated the tunnel floor. Mrs. Bannister was never going to believe this excuse for messy homework.

The girls gave me a strange look as they passed

me kneeling in the mud. I couldn't decide whether to ignore them or tell them what had happened. Either way it was embarrassing—I could look like a jerk who dropped his papers in the mud for no reason, or I could look like a jerk who couldn't defend himself.

They were gone so quickly I didn't have to decide. Now that my fear was beginning to wear off, I was getting really mad. Mad at those creeps for messing around with me. And madder at myself for taking it.

I stuffed my books and papers into the backpack and ran toward town. When I stepped into the daylight, the sun made me blink. There were cars and people on Main Street, but no one paid any attention to me as I walked down the sidewalk. I felt all shaky inside, like I needed to sit down.

The cement steps of the leather shop might be the place to catch my breath. I sat down to rest. The front door was open, and I could hear soft rock music coming from inside. I moved aside to let a customer out, and then Mr. Studebaker sat down next to me.

"Hi," he said. "Haven't I seen you before?"

"Yeah," I said. "I talked to you one day about that white coat in the window."

"Sure. Now I remember." He pulled on one end of his moustache. "I still haven't sold it." He looked me in the eye. "I didn't get your name, did I?"

Since I was resting on his front steps, I decided I

should tell him who I was. Besides, he didn't look nearly as sinister as those weirdos in the tunnel. And right now I needed somebody to talk to.

"Joshua McIntire," I said. I stuck my right hand out, and he grabbed it and gave me a strong shake. My mom says you can tell somebody's character by how they shake hands. If that was the case, then Mr. Studebaker was okay.

"You look a little shook up, Joshua," Mr. Studebaker said. "Anything wrong?"

I didn't know it was so obvious.

He was a good listener. He didn't interrupt or get all excited the way my mom sometimes does. He just listened quietly to the whole story, as though everything I said was really important.

"Well, Joshua," he drawled, "you've had quite a day. I think we'd better call the police."

My heart sank. I'd only been in Grandville for two months, and I'd already met the paramedics from the fire department. Now the police? But Mr. Studebaker seemed to think it was what I should do, and he went inside the store to call them.

The black and white car pulled up in front of the shop right away, and two officers got out. They wore dark sunglasses and their radios were crackling. They looked almost as scary as the guys in the tunnel. But at least Mr. Studebaker was there.

One officer had a clipboard, and he started asking

17

me questions about what happened. I tried to remember exactly what my attackers looked like, and Mr. Studebaker helped me out by reminding me of a couple of things I'd told him.

The policemen seemed to think they knew who the guys were. They'd been in trouble before for bothering some other kids.

"I think we can take care of this problem, Joshua. In the meantime, walk through the tunnel with a buddy," suggested the officer.

The policemen left the shop, and I figured I'd better get home. Mom would be there soon, and I didn't want her to worry.

"What say we call your mom and have her pick you up here?" suggested Mr. Studebaker.

"Naw," I said. "I don't want to bother her. They get mad if she gets calls at work."

"Well, I think this qualifies as a bona fide emergency," he said. "Let me take the responsibility for it."

I was glad to relax and let someone else worry about things for a change.

He called Associated Foods where Mom worked. I could tell that she was all upset at first, but Mr. Studebaker convinced her that I was fine and she could pick me up whenever she got out of work.

"How about a soda pop?" Mr. Studebaker asked.

"Sure," I said. Since he'd spoke to my mom on the

phone, I guessed it was okay to have refreshments.

"And then you can help me around here until your mom comes," Sonny said.

"Thanks, Mr. Studebaker. I'd like that," I said, remembering my manners.

"Call me Sonny. I'm not big on formalities."

I looked around the shop while I finished my pop. Sonny needed a lot of help— there was stuff piled everywhere. As soon as I threw my empty can into the trash, Sonny handed me a broom.

"How about sweeping up the shop?" he asked. "I make a big mess when I cut new leather, and I'm usually too tired at the end of the day to clean up."

My mom had shown me the best way to sweep, and I was careful not to raise a cloud of dust as I moved the leather scraps and dirt into a pile in the center of the shop. The music coming out of the boom box on the counter made me feel energetic. This was fun!

When I'd finished sweeping, I leaned against the wall and watched Sonny cut the leather. "What are you making?" I asked.

"This is going to be a fine coat for a businessman in the city," he answered.

I wondered to myself where he'd learned to sew.

He seemed to read my mind. "My mom taught me how to do this," he said. "Isn't the smell of new leather just great? I never get tired of it."

"How do you know where to cut?" I asked. I hoped I wasn't asking too many dumb questions, but Sonny didn't seem to mind.

"I mark the hides with this pen," he explained. "When I cut out the pieces, the marks just disappear." Then he looked straight at me. "How are you really feeling after your tunnel adventure?"

I wasn't quite sure. I'd been so busy helping Sonny and watching him work that I'd been able to forget about it. But down deep, I was still pretty shook up. I decided to be honest. "I'm kinda scared about running into those guys again," I said.

"You know, when I was in Vietnam, I felt that same way after going out on patrol. I'd meet the enemy and know that I should be brave, but down deep I wanted to cry."

Sonny had described exactly the way I felt. I looked at him with admiration. I'd never known anybody who'd fought in a war before.

"So what did you do?" I asked. I hoped I wasn't being too nosy.

"Well, two things helped me," Sonny said. "First of all, I started praying, and then I took up karate."

I wanted to ask what the two things had to do with each other, but right then my mom came through the door. She rushed over and gave me a big hug, and I turned all red and got embarrassed. Sonny didn't seem to notice.

"I can't believe you, Joshua McIntire," she said. "You sure know how to make a mother worry."

"Aw, Mom," I protested. "It wasn't my fault."

Sonny interrupted. "He's going to be just fine, Mrs. McIntire."

I suddenly remembered my manners. "Mom, this is Sonny Studebaker. Sonny, this is my mom."

They shook hands with each other, and then everything got real quiet. I could tell my mother was trying to figure out what kind of a person Sonny was. His long hair and sandals made her suspicious.

Finally she broke the silence. "Well, I really appreciate your helping Joshua out this afternoon. Lately, he seems to find trouble wherever he goes."

Sonny smiled broadly. "He's just an all-American boy, Mrs. McIntire. I was just the same when I was his age."

He turned and winked at me. "Josh," he continued, "stop by the shop someday after school if you're interested in a little part-time job."

I couldn't believe it. Sonny was offering me a real job!

"Well, we'll talk about it when we get home," my mom said. "Thanks very much for everything, Mr. Studebaker."

"Call me Sonny," he said with a smile. I wasn't sure if he was smiling at me or my mom.

We were both quiet on the way home. I was thinking about my conversation with Sonny, and Mom was probably wondering what could possibly happen next. And then I blurted it out.

"Mom, I need to take karate lessons."

"Karate lessons!" She sounded totally exasperated. "Joshua, why do you spring these things on me when I'm tired and hungry?"

"Then you'd be willing to talk about it after dinner?" I pleaded.

"I suppose so," she said. "But if it costs money, forget it. Our budget is tight."

My heart sank. I'd forgotten about the money part. Then I remembered Sonny's job offer. Maybe I could pay for the lessons myself. But I kept my mouth shut and set the table for dinner.

We were having sloppy joes. My mom puts lots of onions and green pepper in them. I'd missed my after-school snack, and I was really starved.

We'd no sooner finished dinner when the telephone rang. It was Wendell.

"I'm picking you up for Awana at 7:15," he said. Awana was the youth program at Wendell's church.

"Gosh, Wendell, I don't think I can go this week. You're not going to believe what happened to me." I told him about the tunnel attack and how Mr. Studebaker had helped me out. "I think I might start working there," I told Wendell.

"Wow, a real job." He sounded a little jealous. "Will he pay you?"

"I guess so," I said, "or it wouldn't be a job."

"So why can't you go tonight?" he wondered.

"I didn't do my ancestor assignment last night because of the toilet trouble. If I don't do it tonight, Mrs. Bannister will never speak to me again."

"Well, if you don't go to Awana every week, you're going to miss out on attendance points."

"Next week for sure," I promised.

It was just as well I wasn't going to Awana. Not only did I have homework to do, but I had to convince Mom that I needed karate lessons. That's what Sonny said kept him from being afraid in Vietnam. Not that Grandville was quite like Vietnam, but whenever I thought of going through the tunnel again, I got a sick feeling in my stomach. And meanwhile, maybe I'd try prayer, too. It was cheaper than karate lessons.

I'd just settled down to start my homework when the phone rang again. I thought maybe it was Wendell making one last attempt to persuade me to come, but it was my dad. Maybe he knew that I'd been thinking about him really hard for the past couple of days.

"Hi, Josh, ole buddy. How ya doin'?" he asked.

I had tons of stuff I wanted to tell him, but suddenly I was tongue-tied. That seemed to be happening to me a lot lately.

"Josh, are you there?"

"Yeah, Dad, I'm here," I stammered.

"So what's new?" he asked.

"Well, there's a lot, actually," I said. Once I got started telling him about the toilet and the tunnel and the job at Studebaker's, I couldn't stop.

"Sounds like an adventuresome life," he said. "Things aren't that exciting where I am."

"So where are you, Dad?" I asked.

"Well, I haven't really decided where to settle yet, so I don't have an address," he said.

"I wish you'd call more," I said. "I miss you."

"I miss you, too, Joshua."

I decided to go for broke. I might not get another chance to talk to him for awhile. "Dad, do you think you could loan me some money to take karate lessons? I'm getting a job. I can pay you back."

There was silence on the other end of the phone. Finally he spoke.

"I don't think so, Josh. Not just yet. Maybe when I get settled and get a new job, I can start sending you some money."

"Okay, Dad." I shouldn't have asked him.

"I'll call again soon, Josh. Bye."

There was a click and he was gone. And I'd forgotten to ask him about ancestors. Oh, well, I could make something up. Mrs. Bannister would never know the difference.

Tears welled up in my eyes. My mom was watching me from across the room.

"Come over here, Joshua," she said. She gave me a big hug. "Don't worry about your karate lessons. We'll figure out some way to do it."

"I don't care about karate lessons, Mom. I just want Dad to come back."

"Josh, we've got to accept where we are right now and make the best of it."

That wasn't so easy. And it wasn't going to be easy to finish my ancestor assignment, either.

But Mom suddenly came to the rescue. She acted all bright and cheerful, like she wanted to forget about the phone call.

"Let's get this assignment done once and for all," she said. "I've got enough interesting relatives to fill three pages." She laughed out loud. "Who do you want to hear about first—Uncle Oscar? He was an airline pilot and made furniture. Then there was

Uncle Sam, who owned a department store that got blown away in the tornado of '56. My favorite was Uncle Babe. He was a truck driver who dressed up like a clown every chance he got."

I started writing as fast as my mom talked, and before I knew it the assignment was done.

When my alarm went off the next morning, it interrupted a fantastic dream. I was wearing a leather outfit and doing a karate demonstration for a huge crowd. My dad was in the front row clapping really hard.

Wendell asked me to tell the tunnel story all over again when he picked me up for school. When I'd finished, he gave me a funny look. "I can't believe the stuff that happens to you," he said.

"I can't either," I answered. "But I hope it stops. My mom can't take much more excitement."

Mrs. Raymond, the principal, was standing outside our classroom when we filed in. Her forehead was all wrinkled up, and she looked upset.

When we all got to our seats, she started in.

"Class, we've got a problem. Someone is stuffing paper towels down the toilet in the boys' washroom. The toilet overflowed three times yesterday."

I could sympathize. I understood toilet trouble.

"From now on, whenever you use the washroom,

you'll have to sign out and write down the time." She held up a clipboard with a pencil attached. "When we find the person who's responsible for this, he's going to have lots of fun scrubbing the washroom floors and walls after school."

I didn't envy the culprit. I'd had my fill of mopping up after leaky toilets.

The morning passed by quickly. It was amazing how much fun school was when you turned in all of your assignments. When the lunch bell rang, we lined up and waited while Mrs. Bannister passed out tickets for everyone who was having hot lunch. Everybody kept telling me to watch out for the maggots in the corn, but so far I hadn't seen any.

We went through the lunch line and started eating our macaroni and cheese. Wendell leaned over and whispered in my ear. "I think I know who's doing it."

"Doing what?" I replied.

"Shhh," said Wendell. "Do you want the whole world to know what we're talking about?"

I looked a little embarrassed. "Sorry," I said. "What are we talking about?"

"The toilets," he said. "I think I know who's stuffing them."

"Who?" I whispered.

"I think it's Ben," he said.

"Are you going to tell?"

27

"Naw. I don't want to say anything if I don't know for sure."

"Maybe we can catch him," I said.

"We'll have to be careful."

Our conversation was cut short when the monitor blew her whistle and dismissed our table.

After lunch we had computers. It was one of my favorite classes. We got to play games if we finished our reading work early. I booted up my reading software and tried to solve the challenge. All of a sudden, out of the corner of my eye, I saw Ben get up and leave the room.

I looked over toward Wendell. I could tell he was thinking the same thing I was. Mrs. Hamlin was bent over her file cabinet looking for some folders. We left our seats and slipped out of the lab.

The washroom was right across the hall, and we were through the door in a flash. It wasn't one of my favorite places. The custodian tried to fool us into thinking it was a pine forest instead of a bathroom, but he wasn't succeeding. Somebody had written "Mrs. Bannister is buggy" on one of the doors. It was the one that Ben was behind.

Wendell and I looked at each other. He put his finger across his lips, and we listened. It didn't take a genius to figure out what Ben was doing.

I motioned to Wendell, and we went back out into the hallway.

"What are you boys doing out here?" Mrs. Raymond had appeared from nowhere.

I jumped, and my heart sank. I didn't need any more trouble. But Wendell took over.

"We think we've found the person who's stuffing the toilets," he said. "He's in there right now."

Mrs. Raymond gave us a big smile. "Why, thank you, boys. He'll never know I had help in solving this mystery." She knocked on the door and went barreling in.

I could just imagine the look on Ben's face when he came out of his stall and found the principal waiting for him.

We hurried back into the computer lab.

Back in the classroom, after lab, we wrote in our journals. I couldn't decide what to write about, so many things had been happening. Mrs. Bannister always wrote a suggestion on the blackboard in case we were stuck. Today's was: "My best friend is . . ." I decided to use her idea.

My best friend is Danny.

I stopped and looked at the words. They didn't seem quite right. Danny was my best friend back in Woodview. But he hadn't even written me a letter or called since I'd moved. Maybe he wasn't my best friend anymore.

I erased the word "Danny" and wrote "Wendell" instead. But that didn't seem quite right, either.

There were still some things about Wendell that really bothered me. But I kept on writing. Nobody would read it anyhow.

My best friend is Wendell. He's really smart and always seems to be there when I need him. But I'd like him even better if he'd wear some normal clothes once in awhile.

My mind started wandering. Maybe I could get Wendell to wear a T-shirt sometime instead of those awful plaid shirts. . . . The recess bell rang, and I put away my journal, but the idea about Wendell didn't go away. Maybe I could do something about it.

I joined the game of basketball in progress, but people were doing more talking than playing.

"Didja hear what happened to Ben?"

"He got caught red-handed by the principal stuffing paper towels."

"Yeah, he's gonna be scrubbing all the washrooms tonight after school."

"I hear the principal's gonna sit and watch him."

I smiled to myself. There was justice in the world.

After school, Wendell and I walked home together. We scuffed through the leaves that were piling up on the sidewalks. We didn't need the jackets we'd worn in the morning.

I decided to jump right in with my idea before I lost my nerve.

"Wendell, have you ever thought about wearing a T-shirt?" I asked.

He looked at me with surprise. "No," he answered. "Why would I want to do that?"

"Because everybody wears T-shirts," I said. "They're cool."

"So I'm not like everybody else," he replied.

That was the understatement of the century.

"Why don't you just try it once?" I suggested. "They're really comfortable."

He was thoughtful. "Maybe we could make a deal," he suggested.

I wasn't sure what he was talking about.

"If I agree to wear a T-shirt, then you have to do something, too," he said.

The conversation wasn't going quite the way I'd planned it.

"Whaddya have in mind?" I asked.

"You have to promise not to miss Awana next week," he said.

I relaxed. I was planning to do that anyhow.

"Okay, it's a deal," I said. "You wear a T-shirt, and I'll go to Awana."

"One problem, though," Wendell said. "I don't have any T-shirts."

"I'll loan you one," I offered.

Maybe there was hope for Wendell after all.

I could hardly wait to see Wendell wearing the T-shirt I'd loaned him. It was one of my favorites—a Chicago Bears with a big number 34 on the back. Walter Payton used to wear that number when he played for the team.

When the bell rang, I raced to open the door, and there he stood—the new Wendell Hathaway. Well, almost new. He still needed jeans and some gym shoes, but that campaign would have to wait. One step at a time.

"Let's go, Wen," I said. "We don't want to be late."

"I feel weird wearing this shirt," he said.

Not nearly as weird as you looked not wearing the shirt, I thought to myself.

"You look great, Wendell," I answered.

"Are you sure, Joshua?" he asked.

"Trust me, Wendell."

My plan was working. Wendell was one step

closer to being normal. But on the playground, nobody seemed to notice Wendell's new wardrobe. They were too busy playing basketball.

When we got inside to our classroom, we didn't see Mrs. Bannister's familiar face. Instead, there was somebody else at the door—a substitute. Mrs. Bannister was absent.

A buzz went through the class.

"Whaddya say we have a little fun today?"

"Let's sink this sub."

"How about changing our names?"

The substitute didn't notice the commotion in the class. She was creating some of her own, shuffling frantically through the papers on Mrs. Bannister's desk.

"Does anyone know where the seating chart is?" she asked desperately.

I looked over at Ben Anderson. The chart was sticking out of his math book.

"Mrs. Bannister doesn't have one," Mark Bryan told her. He gave Ben a smug smile.

"Well, class, just sit down. We'll make some name tags after I do the lunch count," she said.

The sub didn't look anything like Mrs. Bannister. She was young, thin, very pretty, and she looked like she was dressed for a party. I'd never seen such high heels. Her feet were sure going to be sore by the end of the day.

"Class, write your name on a piece of paper and tape it to the front of your desk. I'll write my name on the board."

She wrote "Ms. Sharon Sheldon" on the blackboard. She must not have known that real teachers never tell kids their first names. Then she began tearing off strips of masking tape and handing them out.

I looked around the room. Nobody was writing their real name on the name tags—except Wendell, of course. You could always count on him to spoil the fun. I was torn. What should I write? I knew that Wendell would expect me to do the right thing, but I didn't want to look like a wimp in front of the rest of the class.

Ms. Sheldon stopped right in front of my desk. My pencil was poised over the paper.

"Are you having trouble deciding who you are?" she asked with a smile.

"N-n-no," I stammered. "I'm Joshua McIntire." My real name tumbled out before I could think. Everyone was staring at me. My face turned a bright red, and I bent over to write my name. Now she was going to think I was the one who was lying.

"Well, Stuart, suppose you tell me what today's math assignment was," Ms. Sheldon began.

Ben Anderson answered her question. "We didn't have an assignment today, Ms. Sheldon."

Ben was Stuart? I was already lost. And we did have a math assignment. Mrs. Bannister always gave math assignments.

Stuart raised his hand, and Ms. Sheldon called on him. "Is that right, Mark?"

Stuart, alias Mark, looked totally confused. He wasn't keeping up with all of this, either, and he couldn't remember what he wanted to say.

"Wendell, can you help us out?" Ms. Sheldon asked.

You could hear the class hold its breath.

"I think somebody forgot that Mrs. Bannister assigned twenty long-division problems for today," Wendell said.

Everyone relaxed. Wendell hadn't blown the whistle on the name changes.

Ms. Sheldon began to read the answers to the division problems. Ben, alias Stuart, stood up.

"Where are you going, Stuart?" asked Ms. Sheldon.

Ben gave her his most winning smile. "I need to sharpen my pencil, Ms. Sheldon," he said sweetly. He took the long way around the room. I wondered what he was up to.

After we graded the papers, Ms. Sheldon asked us to pass them in. I wondered how long it would take her to figure out that nobody was who they said they were. She collected the papers and went back to Mrs. Bannister's desk and sat down.

35

Wendell left his seat and walked to her desk. Every eye was on him. All I noticed was the big 34 on his back. It looked great. But what was he up to? Before he could say anything, Ms. Sheldon tried to stand up. She got a funny look on her face and reached for the back of her skirt. Her expression changed to one of horror, as tears welled up in her eyes.

"This was my first teaching assignment, and it's ruined!" she sobbed. She was crying pretty hard, but we still didn't know what was wrong. Wendell tried to calm her down, but the rest of the class just stared.

We needed help. I didn't even ask permission; I just got out of my seat and ran down to the office. Mrs. Raymond was on the phone. I waited anxiously at the doorway.

"What can I do for you, Joshua?" she asked as she hung up.

"We've got an emergency in our class," I said.

"Is someone hurt?" she asked.

"It's hard to explain. You'd better just come."

We hurried back to the classroom together. Everything looked exactly the same as when I'd left, as though I'd frozen the frame on a VCR. The class was still sitting there staring at Ms. Sheldon. Wendell was still standing next to her desk. And Ms. Sheldon, with tears streaming down her face, was still half standing and half sitting in her chair.

Mrs. Raymond didn't wait to see what would happen next. She moved into action.

"Class, take out something to do and get busy immediately. I don't want to see anyone without work on their desk."

"What's going on here?" she asked Wendell. With my eyes bent to my library book, I tried to hear how Wendell was going to explain this one. I still didn't know what was going on.

Wendell told it all, starting with the name switch and ending with the Crazy Glue that someone had drizzled all over Ms. Sheldon's chair.

Now I knew what Ben had been doing earlier. Poor Ms. Sheldon. She was stuck to that chair forever—at least her dress was.

Mrs. Raymond buzzed the office and issued some orders. "Mrs. Turner, send the custodian to Mrs. Bannister's room. We'll need a new substitute as soon as possible. Meanwhile, tell Mrs. Hamlin to cancel her computer labs and take over here."

Then she turned to the class. "As for you people— I haven't decided yet what's going to happen to you." Her eyes scanned the classroom. "And rip those phony name tags off your desks immediately."

What happened next would make a great movie. The custodian tried to carry the chair with Ms. Sheldon still stuck to it. They looked like some sort of strange circus act. It was almost impossible to keep from laughing, that is, unless you looked at Mrs. Raymond. She looked like a volcano about to erupt. I could tell she was planning something terrible for 5B.

Mrs. Hamlin arrived, and Mrs. Raymond gave her instructions. "This group is not to leave this room for the rest of the day."

Then she faced the class. "I'll be back with your consequences later."

The room went absolutely silent. Everyone found something to do. I watched the hands of the clock move slowly by. This was going to be the longest day of the school year.

I started thinking about the newspaper project Tracy Kendall and I were working on. We were planning to write an editorial about the school lunch program. I decided to get started.

The school lunches at Jefferson are terrible. They are too pale. Everything that is served looks like it has been washed in bleach. Last week we had corn, chicken patties, and pears all at the same time. The cooks need to add some color to the lunch. The vegetables are the worst. Especially the carrots. No one ever eats them. Please don't serve carrots again. And there are maggots in the corn, also. Take the money you spend on corn and carrots and buy something good like M&M's or at least cookies.

I looked at what I had written. I wasn't sure Tracy would like it.

The day dragged by. I would have been glad to

get to the lunchroom today, even for maggoty corn, but we had to eat in our classroom. Mrs. Raymond was serious about grounding us. She came back just before dismissal time. I could tell a lecture was coming.

"Class, you did some serious damage today. You damaged the reputation of Jefferson School, and you hurt the feelings of a brand-new teacher. What's more, you hurt yourselves. It's going to be a long time before I'll be able to trust 5B again."

Mrs. Raymond sure knew how to make a class feel bad.

"I want each of you to write a personal note of apology to Ms. Sheldon. I doubt very much that she'll ever come back to Jefferson School, but at least we can let her know we're sorry. This class will be grounded for the rest of the month—no recess and no assemblies."

No one said a word. We knew we deserved it and more.

Wendell and I walked quietly home. No one had even noticed his T-shirt. I wondered if I was the only one who cared what Wendell wore. What a rotten day.

"Let's stop by the karate place," I suggested to Wendell.

"What for?"

"I want to take lessons," I said.

"Why?"

"So I can defend myself the next time somebody bothers me," I answered.

"How much does it cost?" Wendell asked.

"I don't know," I said. "But my mom said we might be able to work it out."

Master Lee's karate school was in a large storefront, two doors down from the leather shop. There was an oversized picture of a man leaping through the air painted on the front window, which was covered with black paint so you couldn't see in. I wasn't sure what we'd find inside.

The smell reminded me of old gym shoes and wet towels. The practice room was empty, but a small Oriental man was seated at a big desk in a very messy office. He stood up and bowed to Wendell and me. I looked at Wendell, and he was bowing back. I did the same.

"I'm Master Lee," he said. "How may I help you?" He stood waiting for a reply. I'd never seen anything as white as his uniform. He was wearing a black belt around his waist.

Since this was my idea, I guessed I'd better say something. "I want to take lessons," I blurted out.

"Ah, yes," he answered. "Why?" He waited once more.

"I . . . I don't know," I stammered. "I guess I want to be able to fight."

Master Lee smiled ever so slightly. "I cannot

40

teach you my fighting art if you will use it to injure others. The martial arts are for those of good character who wish to learn self-discipline and self-control. Kindness and courtesy are more important than fighting."

I wasn't sure I understood, but I nodded.

"What is your name, young man?" Master Lee inquired.

"Joshua McIntire," I answered.

"Well, young Joshua," he continued, "think about what I have said. If you wish to join our group, I would be happy to have you."

He handed me a brochure and bowed once more. Wendell and I bowed back. We made our way out to the sidewalk. It seemed too bright and noisy after the quiet of Master Lee's office.

"So, what do you think?" I asked Wendell.

"He's really smart," Wendell answered. "I bet he'd be a really good teacher."

I made up my mind. I had to find a way to get karate lessons.

I was glad Mom wasn't home so I could think about everything before she got there. I looked through the karate brochure. There was an introductory offer for $39.95. If I got the leather shop job, maybe I could help.

Mom came home right on time, carrying a big cardboard box.

"Pizza" she said. "We're celebrating."

"Celebrating what?" I asked.

"I got my first raise today," she answered.

"That's terrific," I said. I gave her a high five.

"Don't get excited: it isn't much. But I think we might manage to squeeze out some karate lessons."

"Yippee!" I shouted. "And I can help. I'm going to take that job with Sonny Studebaker."

"Let's talk about it while we have dinner," she said. "Set the table, and we'll dig in."

The gooey cheese and spicy pepperoni tasted even better with the prospect of karate lessons in the offing. For awhile I even forgot that my dad didn't want to help me pay for them.

I told Mom about the substitute teacher.

"I'm proud of you for not changing your name," she said.

"Well, I really didn't plan it that way," I said.

"Even if you didn't, you still made the right choice. How did Wendell look in your T-shirt?"

"The day was so strange, nobody noticed," I said. "Maybe clothes aren't as important as I thought."

"Maybe you're growing up," Mom answered.

"When can I sign up for the lessons?" I asked.

"Why don't you talk to Master Lee and Mr. Studebaker tomorrow night after school? Then we can figure out when you're going to do all of this."

"There's one thing I can't miss," I said, "and that's Awana. I promised Wendell if he wore my T-shirt, I'd go to his club."

"Wendell's folks invited us to church with them again, too," Mom said. "We're going to need a secretary soon to keep track of all our appointments."

I was glad to hear the cheerfulness in her voice. Getting a raise must have made her feel good. Even if my dad didn't appreciate her, people at work did.

At bedtime, I decided to take the other half of Sonny Studebaker's advice. I wasn't quite sure how to do it, so I just started talking.

God, thanks for letting me take karate lessons. Could

You please help me convince Wendell to wear jeans and gym shoes?

I wondered how God could hear me if He was in heaven. I'd have to ask Wendell about that.

And God, watch over my mom. I don't know what I'd do if anything happened to her. Tell my dad to call us more often and come back. And also, God, thanks for the pizza.

How did God keep from getting everybody's prayers mixed up. Another question for Wendell. . . .

I could hardly wait for Friday to end. Mrs. Bannister bawled us out for the way we'd treated the substitute. Then she poured on the work. We worked right through lunch recess and afternoon recess. When the bell finally rang, I reminded Wendell I wouldn't be walking home with him and took off toward town.

I had to make a decision—take the long way round over the tracks or the shortcut through the tunnel. Maybe after a few karate lessons. For now, I didn't mind the extra blocks.

I went to see Master Lee first. He was seated in his office when I entered.

"Ah, young Joshua. How are you today?" He stood up and bowed.

I returned the bow and answered. "Fine, thank you, Master Lee."

"Have you thought about my advice, Joshua?"

"Yes, Master Lee, and I want to take karate lessons," I answered.

"You will learn, Joshua, that karate is hours and hours of hard work and practice. You must discipline your mind as well as your body."

I nodded.

"You will be tempted to quit because what we do seems boring. All you can think of now is what you have seen in the movies. That is not karate."

I didn't care. I just wanted to get started.

"The beginners' class meets on Monday and Wednesday evenings from six to seven."

"I'll be here Monday at six," I said. "My mom will call you to talk about paying."

"Excellent, young Joshua. I will see you then."

I raced out of the school and two doors down to the leather shop. I was so excited that I didn't see Sonny Studebaker coming out of his door, and we ran right into each other.

"Well, if it isn't the human cannonball," Sonny said. "Where are you going in such a hurry?"

"To see you," I said. "Do you still want me to work for you?"

"Of course," he answered.

"I just signed up for karate lessons," I said.

Sonny broke into a big smile. "Great news, Joshua."

"I need to work to help my mom pay for them. I'm lucky I met you," I said.

"Well," Sonny drawled, "I don't think it's luck. I think it's God's will."

I didn't know what he was talking about, and my face must have shown it.

"God works in mysterious ways," Sonny said. "We don't always know why things happen in our lives, but He's got it all planned out."

"Do you mean that God might have sent those guys to bother me in the tunnel?" I asked.

"Well, maybe God wanted you to stop by and visit me, and He couldn't think of a better way for it to happen," Sonny said.

I wondered if God was behind my dad leaving, too. If that was the case, I wasn't sure I trusted Him.

Sonny broke into my thoughts by asking when I wanted to start.

"I've got karate on Monday and Wednesday, and Awana on Tuesday. Maybe I could work a couple hours on Thursdays, Fridays, and Saturdays?"

"Sounds good to me," he said. "On Saturdays you'll have time to help me cut patterns."

I was afraid to ask about money, but Sonny read my mind.

"I'll pay you once a week, on Thursdays. You'll be making $2.50 an hour."

I wasn't going to argue with that amount.

"Do you have time to come in now and learn the ropes?" he asked.

I looked up at the clock on his wall. It was almost five.

"I'd better get home. My mom will be worried. But I'll be back tomorrow morning."

I couldn't wait to tell Mom the good news. She had left some hamburger defrosting in the sink, and I had the meat browning and the table set when she walked in the door.

"Are you feeling all right, Joshua?" she asked.

"Aw, Mom. Just because I'm doing something nice doesn't mean I'm sick."

She laughed and gave me a hug.

"Things are looking up," I said. "Karate lessons start Monday, and I start my job tomorrow."

"I'm impressed, Joshua," she said. "I didn't get my first job until I was sixteen, and here you are with one at ten."

I could tell she was really proud of me.

"Just don't neglect your studies for all of these extra activities, Joshua," she warned. "School is really important. If I'd gone to college, I'd be able to make more money for us today."

"You're doing great, Mom," I reassured her. "You got a raise already, and you've just been working a few months."

I decided to do my homework right after dinner. I'd have to be organized to handle everything. I'd just started my math when the phone rang.

"Hi, Josh. It's Ben."

"Oh, hi," I answered.

"Whaddya doin'?" he asked.

"Finishing my homework," I answered.

"On Friday night? I was wondering if you wanted to go to the movies."

"Gosh, Ben, I don't think so. I'm starting a job tomorrow, and I've got to keep up with my homework or my mom won't let me keep it."

"A job? Where?" He sounded sort of jealous.

"Studebaker's Leather Emporium," I said.

"That guy's strange," Ben said. "My dad says he's a religious nut. Why would you wanna work there?"

Ben's question made me feel funny. I didn't know what to say.

"Well, I've gotta go now, Ben. See you Monday."

Just when I was feeling really good about something, Ben had to come along and spoil it. I tried to forget his comment while I finished the editorial on pale carrots and maggoty corn. Why should Ben's opinion matter? He'd been nothing but trouble for me since I got into town.

My mind began to wander back over the day, and I remembered Sonny's comment about God's will. I wondered if Ben was part of God's will, too. I didn't see how he could be.

Usually on Saturdays I like to lie in bed till nine o'clock and then watch cartoons before I get dressed. But not today. This was the first day of my new job.

Mom was putting in some overtime at the office, and she was ready to go out the door when I came down to the kitchen. I got dressed and fixed my breakfast in record time. I even washed out my cereal bowl and put it back in the cupboard. In our old house we'd had a dishwasher. But then, we had more dirty dishes, too.

I was about to open the front door when the bell rang. It was Wendell wearing, of all things, a T-shirt. And not my Chicago Bears shirt, either—which, I reminded myself, I'd have to remember to get back. I wanted to wear it next week.

Wendell flung his arms open. "So, whaddya think?" he asked.

The shirt was orange and blue with a big Indian chief on the front.

49

"Turn around and let me see the back," I said.

In orange letters across the back it said "University of Illinois."

"What's the University of Illinois?" I asked.

"That's where I want to go to college," said Wendell.

I myself was hoping to make it through fifth grade.

"So, whaddya think?" he asked again.

"Wendell, you are awesome," I said.

"Does that mean you like it?" he said with a laugh.

"Absolutely," I said. "Next thing you know, you'll be wearing gym shoes." I hoped I wasn't pushing him too fast. "Wendell, sorry I can't hang around. Don't wanna be late on my first day on the job!" We went down the porch steps together and then parted ways.

Sonny was helping a lady when I got to the shop. She smelled like a perfume factory. He smiled and motioned me behind the counter. I put my jacket on a stool and stood quietly waiting while he showed the lady various coat styles from a book.

"Why don't you grab some pop from the fridge?" he said. "I'll be right with you."

The cold soda felt good going down. I'd run almost the whole way, and I was thirsty. I looked around the shop. There were piles of leather everywhere. I wondered how Sonny found anything in this mess. Maybe that's why he needed help.

Music was coming from the boombox, and even though it sounded like rock 'n roll, the musicians were singing about Jesus.

Sonny was finished with the customer. He stuck out his hand and gave me another one of those firm handshakes. "Welcome aboard, Joshua," he said. "I'm glad that you're working for me."

"Thanks," I replied. "I hope I'm okay."

"You'll be fine," he answered. "That's why I hired you. I'm a good judge of character."

I put my soda down on the counter.

"You're about to learn your first lesson," he said. "We never put anything on the counter that might damage the skins. They're very expensive." He took my can off the counter and put it on a low shelf against the wall.

"I'm sorry," I said. I wondered if he was going to change his mind about hiring me, but he went right on as if nothing had happened.

"Let's figure out what you're going to do each day. I think we'll write up a little job description for you." He took a pencil stub from behind his ear and started writing on the back of an envelope.

"First you'll sweep the floor. Then you can straighten the skins. They get messy when I show them to people. Stack them in piles by size."

I was glad he was writing all of this down.

"Then when you finish with that, you can fold up the patterns I've finished using." He handed me the crumpled envelope.

The morning flew by. I didn't even have time to think. At noon Sonny said, "Time to head for home, Josh. I'll see you next week."

I remembered how I used to skip down the sidewalk in first grade. I was too old to do that now, but I sure felt like it. I was earning money, and I would have my first karate lesson on Monday.

Mom was opening a can of soup when I got home. Chicken noodle. I was really hungry.

"How was work?" we both asked at once, then laughed. It felt good.

I told her all about my job description and how hard I'd worked.

"I called Master Lee today," she said. "You're all set for three months of lessons."

Three months sounded like a long time.

"You'll need a uniform," she said. "Master Lee said you can pay for it a little bit at a time out of your earnings. You'll get it at your first lesson."

I hoped it would be as white as Master Lee's. I was so excited I didn't think I'd be able to sleep that night, but I must have drifted off right in the middle of my prayers. The last thing I remember saying was, "Thanks, God, for letting me take karate. Please make Dad call soon."

Even though we went to church with Wendell's family, Sunday dragged by. On Monday, I woke before the alarm rang. I could hear Mom getting ready. I jumped out of bed and ran out to the kitchen.

"My goodness, what are you doing up so early?" she said. "You could sleep for another half-hour."

"I'm just excited," I said.

"Well, don't get so excited you forget to pay attention in class. Those grades have to stay up if you're going to stay in karate."

"They will. I promise, Mom."

"As long as you're up, you can make your own lunch. I'm running a little late."

As I spread chunky peanut butter on bread, I thought about my prayer of the night before. I wondered if God could really make my dad call.

When I got to school, everybody was talking about the Jefferson Masquerade. The librarian had a special display of books about costumes, really fancy stuff and the easy make-your-own kind. Even Mrs. Bannister was getting in the spirit of things. She'd hung a bunch of neat looking masks across the top of the chalkboard.

But I couldn't even keep my mind on costumes and parades. I was too busy watching the hour hand inch slowly toward three o'clock. I couldn't think of anything but karate.

We worked in groups on a social studies project,

took a science test, and worked on our autobiographies. Mine was coming along pretty well. Once the dismissal bell finally rang, I decided to stop by the public library on the way home from school. I wanted to see if they had any books on karate.

The library was small and packed full of books. I went downstairs to the children's section and looked in the card catalog. I was glad I'd listened in library skills class. Only one karate book was in. The librarian helped me find it, and I checked it out.

The King Kone hadn't closed for the season yet, so I treated myself to a Mister Frosty with M & M's and looked through the book. The pictures were great. I read every word of the chapter on kicking techniques. The author said kicking should be used "only in case of danger." I decided my tunnel experience qualified as danger.

I heard the courthouse clock striking five. I needed to hustle to get home and then back to Master Lee's before six. I ran almost the whole way.

Mom was making a ham sandwich for me when I ran up the back steps. "You won't have time for a big dinner tonight," she said.

I didn't dare tell her I wasn't hungry. She didn't approve of Mister Frostys before dinner. I took a few bites and swallowed some milk.

"Are you nervous, Joshua?" she asked.

"Naw, Mom," I said. "I'm fine." But I wasn't

really. I'd never been so excited in my life.

"I'll take you to class," she said.

"I can walk," I protested.

"It'll be dark before you finish," she said. "Besides, I want to see what the place looks like."

I didn't mind. I was pretty tired from running all the way home. I needed my strength for kicking.

There were half a dozen people of different ages and sizes warming up. Master Lee bowed to my mom and handed me a white uniform.

"This is your *gi*, young Joshua," he said. "You can change in the room at the back, then sign in." He pointed to a clipboard on the counter. "Each evening when you come, write your name and the date."

I took my uniform and white belt and left my mom talking to Master Lee. When I got back, she was gone.

"Your mother will return at seven o'clock when your lesson is over," Master Lee explained. "Come, we are ready to begin."

I didn't see anyone I knew, but that was just as well. If I goofed up during my first lesson, I didn't want anyone to know it.

Master Lee stepped onto the mat, and everyone stopped what they were doing and started lining up.

"We are lining up in order of rank, young Joshua," explained Master Lee. "You are the newest student and will be the last."

Then everyone bowed. I got in on the bow a little late, but next time I'd know what was happening. Then Master Lee bowed to the group. Then everyone bowed to the flag on the wall and to the picture of a fierce looking Oriental man.

I didn't know about all this bowing stuff, but my book said it took the place of shaking hands in Japan.

"Now we will begin our warm-up exercises," said Master Lee.

Everyone hit the mat and began doing push-ups. I was glad I'd been working on physical fitness in gym class. It would come in handy here. The perspiration was dripping down my back, and I could feel my face turning red.

After the warm-ups, Master Lee gave instructions to the rest of the class to practice their forms, and he took me aside. "Now, Joshua, are you ready to learn about *kiai*?"

I didn't have any idea what *kiai* was, but I nodded.

"*Kiai*," he explained, "is the karate shout."

All right. We were going to do the best part first.

"You make this short, sharp yell to show determination, concentration, and effort," said Master Lee. "As you exhale, Joshua, you will shout the words 'huh' or 'uts'. This will tighten your stomach muscles and give more power to your technique. Now, let me hear you practice the kiai," he said.

I'd seen this enough times on TV, but now that I was supposed to do it, I was embarrassed.

"Don't be shy," Master Lee encouraged. "Make the sound."

I sounded pitiful. Sort of like a kitten mewing.

"Try once more, young Joshua."

I remembered my tunnel experience and gave a mighty shout.

"Excellent. Now we will learn how to stand."

The hour passed quickly as Master Lee demonstrated the horse stance. "Notice how my toes are pointed outward and my body is in the semi-squat position," said Master Lee. "You may feel uncomfortable at first, but if you practice diligently, your legs will become very strong."

I could see why they called it the horse stance. Master Lee looked like he was riding.

When class was over, everyone bowed again. I hadn't noticed my mom slip in. I grabbed my clothes, and we headed for the car.

"How about a cold drink?" she asked. "You really look thirsty." She pulled the car into the King Kone parking lot. "What'll it be?" she asked.

"I'll have a root beer," I said. I hadn't felt this good since we moved to Grandville.

On Thursday morning I was practicing the horse stance and karate shout before school. It was a lot easier doing it alone in my living room than in front of Master Lee and the class. The phone rang, startling me. No one called in the morning. It was Wendell.

"I'm not going to school today," he reported. "I've got the flu. Will you pick up my homework?"

"Sure," I said. "But I work after school today. I'll bring it by after supper. Hope you feel better."

I started off for school, but I missed Wendell. I'd grown to depend on him. We always talked about kids in the class and stuff we were thinking about. I was even getting used to his clothes.

Today Wendell would miss moving our desks into new cooperative groups. Mrs. Bannister assigns the kids to each group, but we get to pick our own team name and decide how to arrange our desks.

I was going to miss my old group, "The Great

58

Brains." Tracy had gotten to be a pretty good friend, and Sondra was okay, too. And Wendell, of course, had turned out to be all kinds of things I'd never expected. But Mrs. Bannister didn't care whether you liked the people in your group or not. She said you had a responsibility to work together no matter what. If you disagreed, she made you work it out.

"Group one will sit over here," Mrs. Bannister announced, pointing to the far corner of the room. "Joshua McIntire, Ben Anderson, Samantha Sullivan, and Maria Lopez."

I couldn't believe my rotten luck. Maria was okay. She was pretty and quiet. But Ben was trouble with a capital "T," and Samantha never shut up. She bossed everybody around. I bet her old group was giving a silent cheer at this very moment. I'd go crazy for the next six weeks.

"Joshua," Mrs. Bannister said, "you can move your desk now."

Just when life was looking up, Mrs. Bannister had to do this to me. Maybe this was her revenge. She was going to pay me back for the cockroaches by slowly torturing me to death.

I figured I'd sit next to Maria and let Ben and Samantha fight it out, but Samantha never gave me a chance.

"Joshua, put your desk right here next to mine," she ordered.

I gave her a dirty look, but it didn't have any effect. Samantha was going to organize my life for the next six weeks. We were supposed to choose our group name together, but Samantha didn't know the meaning of the word cooperation.

"I've got our name all picked out," she announced with authority. "Bannister's Babies."

"That's dumb," I said. "We're not babies."

"But it sounds good," she said. "I like it."

"Well, what about the rest of us?" I asked.

"Everybody else likes the name. Don't you?" She directed her question to Ben and Maria. They didn't say a word. "See?" she said. "It's all settled."

Bannister's Babies. It was the stupidest name I'd ever heard. And nobody even cared. I decided that if Samantha was going to run the group, she could do it without me. I was going on strike.

"I'm not going to be in this group if that's the name," I said.

"Mrs. Bannister," Samantha screeched. "Joshua isn't cooperating at all."

Mrs. Bannister walked over to our group. "Sometimes it takes a while for a group to get organized. I'm sure you'll work it out."

She was dead wrong. I'd never work anything out with Samantha Sullivan.

By the time the day ended, I'd had about all I could stand of Samantha. "Joshua, do this. Joshua, do that. Joshua, you're not listening to me."

I'd have to get up the courage to ask Mrs. Bannister about moving me to a new group. But for now, I'd forget about school. I had to go to work.

Sonny was sewing at the big machine when I got there. The boombox was turned up loud, and he was tapping his foot in time to the music.

"Isn't this a great song, Joshua?"

"I guess so," I said. "I've never heard it before."

"This is my group," he said. "That's me playing the drums." He turned up the bass, and the floor seemed to shake. Then he laughed and turned it back down. "We're called 'The King's Messengers,' " he said. "We've got a concert at the community college Saturday night. How about going along?"

"I'd have to ask my mom," I said.

"I'd be glad to talk to her. Think about it. You could take a friend."

I wondered if Wendell would feel up to a rock concert. I grabbed the broom and began sweeping. Sonny started sewing again. The music played softly in the background. This was really peaceful compared to my day with Samantha. She was going to ruin my life if I couldn't get moved.

I swept the leather scraps into a dustpan and dumped them into the trash. Then I took the trash can out the back door. The railroad tracks ran behind the shop, and a freight train was rumbling by. It reminded me of my adventure on the tracks with Ben. How could I be in a "cooperative group" with a guy who had deserted me, leaving me lying by the tracks with a broken leg?

Back in the shop, I began to stack the pieces of leather. Sonny asked how school had gone, and before I knew it I had spilled the whole story.

"Sounds like you've got your work cut out for you," he said. "Samantha's going to be a real challenge."

"Well," I said, "I can't stand her, and I won't work with her."

"Do you have a choice?" Sonny asked. "Besides, you can't always tell a book by its cover. Maybe Samantha's really a nice person inside."

Sonny sounded like my mom. That was what she'd said about Wendell when I first met him—and she'd been right. But Samantha was another story. She was definitely a pain, inside and out.

I finished up the last of my chores and grabbed my stuff.

"Shall I call your mom tonight about the concert?" Sonny asked.

"That sounds great," I said. "If she says okay, I'll invite Wendell, my next-door neighbor."

When I got home, Mom was taking meatloaf and

baked potatoes out of the oven. I'd worked up an appetite, and I demolished three slices with chili sauce in a hurry. I was working on a piece of apple pie when I remembered Sonny's invitation.

"Mom, Sonny Studebaker is going to call and invite Wendell and me to a rock concert Saturday night at the college," I announced.

She raised an eyebrow. "Aren't you a little young for rock concerts?"

"Sonny plays in this group," I explained. "They play Christian music. Wendell knows all about it."

"I'll check it out with Mr. Hathaway and let you know," she said. "Don't you have to get a costume together for school sometime soon?"

I couldn't believe it. I'd completely forgotten about the Jefferson Masquerade, I'd been too busy.

"I've got to take Wendell his homework," I said. "He was out with the flu today. Maybe he'll have an idea about costumes."

Wendell was a lot better. "I've been watching TV all day and drinking 7-Up," he told me.

Huh. While I'd been fighting off Samantha Sullivan, he'd had a great day.

"You're not going to believe our new groups," I said. "I've got to put up with Samantha."

"Wow," said Wendell. "That's going to be a real challenge."

Wendell never said anything bad about anybody—

but even he recognized that Samantha was totally impossible.

"Hey," I said, suddenly remembering Sonny's invitation. "How would you like to go to Sonny's rock concert with me at the college Saturday night?"

"That would be neat," said Wendell. "How would we get there?"

"Sonny invited us," I said. "I think that means he'll drive."

"I don't know," said Wendell. "My folks are real fussy about who I can ride with."

"My mom's going to talk to your dad," I said. "The other important thing is the Jefferson Masquerade. What are you gonna be?"

"I don't know," said Wendell. "Maybe I'll go as a mummy. I can just roll up in my bed sheet like I've been doing all day."

"I did that once," I said. "It was fun."

"Then it's settled," said Wendell. "I'll go as a mummy. What about you?"

I suddenly made up my mind. "I'm going to wear my karate uniform," I said.

"Sounds good," he said. "See you tomorrow."

Somehow Sonny, my mom, and Wendell's dad worked it all out. At seven o'clock Saturday night we were in Sonny's van on our way to the community college field house. There was hardly room for us with all of the drums and amplifiers.

The field house was starting to fill up when we got there. Sonny unloaded all of his equipment backstage and got us settled in our front-row seats.

"You guys stay right here. Don't move until I come for you after the concert," Sonny said. "I'll wave from the stage."

I'd never heard live music before. We watched the stage hands setting up microphones and amplifiers. Guys with long hair were testing guitars and shouting back and forth. They didn't seem to be very organized. All of sudden the lights went dim, and the crowd began to applaud. Wendell and I joined in. A voice came over the loudspeakers announcing "The King's Messengers," and the spotlight hit the stage.

"There's Sonny!" I shouted. I could see him near the back of the stage. He was twirling his drumsticks and bobbing his head. His long hair was tied back in a ponytail. Everybody was clapping and singing along. They must have heard the song before. It was all about love and Jesus, and the crowd was swaying back and forth.

When the song ended, Wendell and I clapped and screamed. The next song was quieter, and everyone sat down. The words this time were about following God's will. I remembered my conversation with Sonny. Maybe he had written this song.

I lost track of all the songs they sang, but suddenly it was time for intermission. Sonny came down and talked to us. He looked hot, and his shirt was soaked with perspiration.

"Drumming is hard work," he said. "What do you guys think of the concert?"

"It's great," I said.

"Yeah," said Wendell. "I've never heard anything like this."

"We're almost done playing," said Sonny. "Then there'll be a speaker."

"Are we having a sermon?" asked Wendell.

"Not exactly a sermon," said Sonny. "But someone is giving their testimony."

"What's a testimony?" I asked.

"When something great happens to someone, they want to tell other people about it," Sonny explained. "That's a testimony."

The lights dimmed a couple of times, and Sonny jumped back up on the stage. "So long for now, guys. Remember to sit tight after the show."

He barely made it back to his drums before the spotlight came back on and the band started to play. I'd heard this one before—"Amazing Grace." They'd sung it at Wendell's church, but it sounded different with guitars and drums.

There were three more numbers, and then the speaker came out, and the crowd went crazy.

"Hi, everybody. I'm Brent Hillman."

Sonny hadn't told us that Brent Hillman was coming. Brent was a star quarterback for the Chicago Bears. No wonder there were so many people here.

"I'm here tonight to tell you about something that has made my life worth living."

Hadn't Brent Hillman's life always been worth living? I wondered. He made over a million dollars a year and had his own sports show.

". . . I decided to turn my life over to Jesus and let Him be the boss. Now whenever I have a problem, I don't need to worry about it."

That sounded like a good deal. I had plenty of problems I'd be glad to turn over to someone else.

" . . . We all think we're pretty cool," Brent was saying. "But actually we're all sinners. We need to ask for forgiveness and believe."

Well, I thought Brent Hillman was definitely cool. If he recommended Jesus, I'd have to give it some serious thought.

Brent talked a little longer, and then he said, "If you've got questions and want to talk with someone, come up to the front afterwards. The people with badges will be glad to help you."

Then he was gone. The lights came on, and people starting moving in every direction. I remembered Sonny's warning and sat tight, but inside I was thinking hard about what Brent Hillman had said.

I'd promised Wendell I'd go to church with him, but when the alarm rang at eight o'clock, I was tempted to turn it off and roll over. Then I remembered Brent Hillman's testimony and decided that maybe going to church wouldn't be such a bad idea after all. Maybe somebody there could answer some questions for me.

The sun was shining, and I could smell bacon frying.

"Good morning, handsome," Mom said when I came into the kitchen. "How shall I do your eggs?"

"Sunny-side up," I said.

"How come you're in such a good mood?"

"Oh, I don't know. I had a great time at the concert last night."

"Tell me more about it," she said.

"Well, like I told you last night, Brent Hillman was there."

"Tell me again. Who is this Brent Hillman?"

I groaned. "Mom, everybody knows who Brent Hillman is. He's the best quarterback in the pros."

"Sorry, Joshua. I'll try to do better next time."

I told her some of the same stuff I'd told her the night before, but she didn't seem to mind that I was repeating myself.

"So how was Sonny?" she asked.

"Really cool," I said. "He's a great drummer."

Why she was so interested in Sonny? I was about to ask her when she glanced at the clock.

"We'd better get ready. The Hathaways are picking us up for church at nine."

I wolfed down the rest of my bacon and eggs and ran to get dressed.

I had a hard time paying attention during the sermon. I was tired from being up late the night before, and I wished Brent Hillman was talking instead of the boring minister. The best part of the service was the little kids' choir that sang during the offering. They were completely off-key, and one little boy kept waving to his mother.

Mom invited Wendell over for lunch. We had hot dogs and potato chips. I thought maybe he'd miss the big roast beef dinner his mother cooked every Sunday, but he must have told my mom how delicious lunch was about ten times.

"You must really like hot dogs, Wendell," my mom said.

"Oh, boy, do I ever, Mrs. McIntire," he gushed. "We never have them at home. My dad can't stand the sight of them."

Wendell and I went out to the back yard after lunch. There was an old tire swing tied to the apple tree, and we took turns seeing how fast we could whirl each other around.

"I think I'm getting sick," Wendell said as he flopped down on the grass. "Show me some karate."

"I haven't learned much yet," I said.

"Show me anyhow."

I showed him the horse stance. "The best part is the shout," I told him. I gave a short, sharp yell in my loudest voice. "HUH!"

Wendell jumped. "Wow," he said. "You sure scared me."

I did it again. "HUH!"

"What's going on over there?" asked a quavery voice. A little white-haired lady peered over the picket fence that separated our yards.

"We're just practicing karate," said Wendell.

"Well, for goodness' sakes. It sounded like someone was getting murdered," she said. "I'm trying to take an afternoon nap."

"I'm sorry," I said. "Let's go inside, Wendell."

"Naw, I'd better head for home. I've got to do my homework from Friday." He vanished through the hedge.

I went inside and flipped on the TV. I'd forgotten the Bears were playing. Brent Hillman had just caught a pass. What a fantastic football player! I started thinking again about what he'd said at the concert. Maybe I'd have a chance to ask Sonny about it next time I saw him.

I was in the middle of a crazy dream when the alarm rang Tuesday morning. I was sitting in a desk that was too small for me, and the teacher was Samantha Sullivan. It was actually more like a nightmare. I woke up hoping it wasn't too late to convince Mrs. Bannister to let me change groups.

Samantha didn't even wait for school to start. She spied me on the playground and zoomed in like a dive bomber.

"Joshua, I've figured out what we should do for our group's slogan. 'Bannister's Babies are the Best.' "

I looked at her. She was unbelievable.

"Samantha, just shut up, will you?"

"Well, you aren't in a very good mood today," she said walking off with her nose in the air.

The bell rang, and I was tempted to turn around and go home. But that wouldn't solve my problem.

Nothing slowed Samantha down for long. She started right in on me once I sat down.

"Joshua, you're going to have to keep your desk

neater if we're going to get the maximum number of group points."

"Lay off, will you, Samantha? I don't even wanna be in your group," I snarled.

I got out of my seat and marched up to Mrs Bannister's desk.

"Mrs. Bannister," I begged, "please move me to another group. It's not going to work with Samantha and me."

"I'm sorry, Joshua, I can't," she explained. "You know the rules. The groups stay together until they work it out."

I was trapped.

Samantha gave me a smug smile. "I know what you're up to, Joshua," she said. "You're just trying to get moved. Well, I'll show you."

She grabbed at my backpack, and I punched her in the arm.

"Ow!" she screeched, and I knew I'd made a terrible mistake. But it was too late. Mrs. Bannister was standing in front of my desk.

"What's going on over here?" she asked.

"Joshua hit me," Samantha wailed.

Mrs. Bannister looked me directly in the eye. "Is that true, Joshua?"

I nodded miserably.

"I'm really disappointed in you, Joshua," she said. "Hitting one of your classmates."

Why do adults always say things like that? You already feel bad enough, and then they rub it in.

"I'm afraid you'll have to see the principal, Joshua," she said.

"Aw, Mrs. Bannister. I'm sorry. I didn't mean it," I pleaded.

"It's too late, Joshua. You broke one of our Jefferson rules."

I felt like the room was closing in on me. How could I have been so dumb?

Wendell looked sympathetically at me across the classroom, but there was nothing he could do.

"Go to the principal's office right now," Mrs. Bannister instructed.

I knew Mrs. Raymond would call my mom. I stepped out into the hall. The door to the playground was still open. I didn't stop to think, I just slipped out the door and ran across the blacktop.

I needed to talk to somebody. It was too late to go back into school. Then I thought of Sonny. I ran toward town.

The bell jangled when I opened the door. Sonny turned from the sewing machine and looked up.

"Hey, Joshua, what are you doin' here? Don't you have school?"

I stared at the floor.

"Hey, buddy, what's goin' on?"

I tried to tell him, but the words wouldn't come

out. The only sound I heard was my own sobbing. And I didn't even care.

Sonny came around the counter and put his hand on my shoulder. I cried even harder.

He pulled a crumpled handkerchief from his pocket and handed it to me. "Just get it all out, Joshua. It's okay to cry."

Finally I told him what had happened.

"You're upset about a lot of stuff, aren't you?" Sonny asked.

All of it came tumbling out. My dad, moving, hearing Brent Hillman. I was really all goofed up inside, but that didn't seem to bother Sonny. He was calm and patient.

"Joshua, the first thing we have to do is call Mrs. Raymond and tell her you're okay," he said. "We don't want her getting your mom all upset."

Mom! I had forgotten about her.

Sonny was on the phone in a flash. I heard him telling Mrs. Raymond what had happened. "Joshua's going to get calmed down, and we'll have him back at school in time for lunch," he promised.

He hung up and turned to me. "Good news, Josh," he said. "They hadn't called her yet. They were still searching the school."

I pictured everyone looking in closets and empty rooms for Joshua McIntire.

Sonny leaned against the counter. "Joshua, I have

a suggestion to make. You don't have to take it. And it won't make all your problems disappear."

I listened intently.

"You need to stop trying to handle everything by yourself," he said. "How about asking Jesus into your life to help you out?"

"Is that what Brent Hillman was talking about the other night?" I asked.

"It sure was," said Sonny. "You can do the same thing Brent did—ask Jesus to forgive you for all of the dumb things you've ever done, and put Him in charge of your life."

"But how do you do that?" I wondered aloud.

"It's real simple," said Sonny. "I did it when I was in Vietnam. You just tell Jesus you need Him and ask Him to start being a part of your life."

I smiled a little and sat up straighter.

"But don't get the idea that all your problems are going to evaporate," said Sonny. "It's just that you'll have Someone to help you get through them."

He locked up the shop and we climbed into his van. I didn't say a word as we drove back to Jefferson. I thought he was just going to drop me off, but he parked the car and came in.

The school building looked different to me. Maybe because Sonny was with me.

Mrs. Raymond was walking down the hall, and Sonny stuck out his hand and introduced himself.

"Could I see you for a few minutes alone?" he asked her.

They disappeared into her office, leaving me alone on the wooden bench outside. The fourth grade class went by on their way back from gym. They looked at me curiously. Nobody sat on that bench unless he was in trouble.

The secretary walked by on an errand and raised her eyebrows. "What are you doing here, Joshua?" she asked.

I shrugged my shoulders. It was too complicated to explain.

Mrs. Raymond and Sonny came out of her office. They shook hands once again.

"I'll see you later, pal," Sonny said. "Think about what I said." He was gone.

Mrs. Raymond motioned me into her office. "I think we've had this conversation before, Joshua," she said.

I nodded.

"Mr. Studebaker and I had an interesting discussion. He seems to think you've learned your lesson."

I nodded again.

"I'm not quite convinced of that myself."

I waited.

"He seems to think that I don't need to call your mother," she said.

I nodded really hard.

"I'm not quite convinced of that either."

I felt like I was on a seesaw.

"But I have seen some positive signs. You used some very good judgment the day the substitute teacher was here."

I was back on the top again.

"One thing is clear, you'll have to have some consequences. What do you think would be appropriate?" she asked.

"I guess I'll have to apologize to some people," I said.

"That's good for a starter. But I'm afraid a little more will be required."

"Maybe I should lose some privileges," I said.

"Or maybe you should perform some service for the school," she suggested.

"Like what?" I asked.

"Well, there's trash to pick up on the playground," she said. "You'll have to do that during all of your recess periods for a week."

I imagined myself picking up trash while everyone stood around and watched. Especially Samantha Sullivan.

"Is it settled then?" she asked.

I nodded for the last time and went back to my class.

Somehow I made it through the rest of the afternoon. Samantha and I ignored each other and nobody said anything about what happened. I was thinking about my conversation with Sonny.

At journal writing time, I picked up my pencil and started writing.

I hate this school. I hate my dad. I hate Samantha Sullivan. I hate everything.

I stopped for a minute. That wasn't really true. I loved my mom. I really liked Sonny. I thought karate was terrific. I just needed some help with my problems. I remembered Sonny's suggestion about telling Jesus you need Him and asking Him to be a part of your life. I closed my eyes and whispered the words to myself.

Only a few seconds had passed, but I felt different. I looked at the words on my journal page. I ripped out the page and crumpled it up.

"Joshua, get to work," Mrs. Bannister said. "You

need to have something in your journal before recess."

I picked up my pencil again and started to write.

I've just decided to be a Christian and I feel great.

I smiled to myself. It was a great day after all.

Mrs. Raymond met me at the door when the recess bell rang. She held out a pair of heavy gloves and some garbage bags. "You might as well get started today, Joshua."

Everyone else was playing basketball, and I was picking up broken glass and trash that had blown against the fence. But I didn't mind. I felt like I could handle anything.

After school I ran all the way to the leather shop. I burst in the door with such enthusiasm that I startled Sonny.

"Is this the same Joshua McIntire that I dropped off at Jefferson School?" he wondered.

I stopped for a second and then answered. "No, I don't think it is."

"What do you mean?" asked Sonny.

"Well, I thought about everything you said and decided to take your advice," I said.

Sonny broke into a wide smile. "Does this mean what I think it means?" he asked.

"Yeah," I answered. "I asked Jesus into my life."

Sonny shouted "Yippee!" and gave me a high five. "That's the best news I've had in a long time. This calls for a celebration."

He grabbed his keys, locked up the shop, and we walked over to King Kone. I had my usual Mister Frosty. It was the best tasting Mister Frosty I'd ever had.

I walked Sonny back to the shop and then headed for home, wondering how I'd tell my mom about everything that had happened today. I wasn't sure she'd understand.

"You're awfully quiet, Joshua," Mom said after supper. "Are you feeling well?" She put her hand on my forehead.

"I don't know," I said. "I'm supposed to go to Awana with Wendell. I promised."

"I think you have a fever. Maybe you're coming down with what Wendell had. I'll call and tell him you can't go."

I was glad to climb into bed. I lay awake in the darkness thinking about my big decision, about what I would do with Samantha, and about my dad. Whenever I started thinking, I always came back to him. I still didn't understand why he wasn't with us.

I whispered a prayer as I drifted off to sleep.

Wednesday night. Time for my fourth karate lesson. I ran home after school and grabbed a quick snack. There was leftover chocolate cake, and I polished off a big piece. Then I put on my karate uniform and went out to the back yard to practice. I was just getting ready to do my shout when I remembered the lady next door. I did a silent shout instead.

"We've got a problem tonight," Mom said during dinner. "I've got to go back to work to finish up a project. I can't pick you up from karate."

"Oh, I can walk home," I said. "It's not far."

"But it'll be dark," she said.

"I'll be okay," I assured her. "I know karate."

She dropped me at Master Lee's at six. I signed in just in time. Everyone lined up in order and did all of their bowing. Then we went through the warm-up exercises. I felt stronger and more agile every time.

As usual, Master Lee left the rest of the group to practice their forms and took me aside.

"Tonight, young Joshua, we are going to learn some kicking techniques."

Oh, boy, I thought to myself. This is really karate.

"Kicking gives a smaller person many advantages in self-defense," Master Lee explained. "But you will never use your kicking to start a fight. Kicking is only used to protect yourself against an attacker."

Master Lee demonstrated two kicks and left me to practice.

"Do them slowly, young Joshua," he reminded from across the room. "Pretend you are in slow motion."

I did it over and over again. It was beginning to get boring, and I was tired.

Master Lee must have known what I was thinking.

"There is an old karate proverb," he said. "One technique mastered is more valuable than one hundred techniques sampled."

I wasn't sure I understood, and it must have shown on my face.

"It is better to practice and know one kick very well than to rush through many without learning them well," he explained.

The class ended, and Master Lee put his hand on my shoulder. "Well done, Joshua. Do not grow discouraged. With practice you will become strong."

I put on my gym shoes and headed down the dark sidewalk. I'd told Mom I'd be okay, but the shadows were scary. I passed the leather shop. There was a single light bulb burning in the back, but Sonny wasn't there. I wondered where he lived and what he did after work.

The King Kone was closed, too. The weather was getting cool. Soon they'd be closed for the season. Now the lights from town faded away. There was a vacant lot, and a possum slithered in front of me across the sidewalk. I jumped out of my skin. Maybe if I ran, I wouldn't get as scared.

Suddenly two figures loomed out of the darkness. I recognized them right away, and my heart stopped. The giants in leather jackets and jeans.

"Hey, look who's here," the pimply one said.

"It's our old friend from the tunnel," said the other.

"And look what he's wearing. Are you gonna be a karate star?" said Pimples.

I wasn't planning on using my karate this soon. But I suddenly felt a burst of courage. I'd been practicing my kick all night. Why not see if it worked? Then I remembered what Master Lee had said about only using karate to defend oneself. I wondered if this qualified.

Pimples helped me make up my mind. He moved closer and tried to shove me.

I took a deep breath, gave a karate shout, and executed a perfect front kick. Practice had paid off.

I hadn't even touched him, but Pimples backed off. Way off.

"Okay, kid, you don't need to get all riled up. I was only kidding."

My heart was beating like a jackhammer, but at least I wasn't paralyzed like before.

"Let's go," Pimples said to his companion. "We've got better things to do."

He didn't fool me. I'd scared him. Even though there were two of them and they were older and bigger, I'd stood my ground. Without even touching them! It was amazing.

I remembered what I'd read in one of the karate books I'd checked out. It said that the *kiai*, the karate shout, was often all that was needed to frighten people off. Those guys were really cowards.

But once they were gone, I started to shake. I looked up at the starry sky and whispered a prayer. Thanks, God, for watching over me. I was just like Sonny. I used karate and prayer.

I ran the rest of the way home. Mom had left the key under a flowerpot, and the porch light was lit. I let myself in and collapsed on a kitchen chair.

Wow. The Grandville chapter of my autobiography would make a good movie. Back in Woodview, I was a pretty normal, dull kid. Now I couldn't keep up with all the excitement.

I took a shower and put on my pj's. The phone rang, and I jumped a mile. I wished Mom would get home. But it was Mom on the phone.

"Josh, are you okay?" she asked.

"Sure, Mom. Why wouldn't I be okay?"

"Oh, I don't know. I had a funny feeling."

"I'm fine," I reassured her. I'd tell her the story when she got home.

"I'll be on my way in twenty minutes. 'Bye."

I climbed into bed and read some more of my karate book. I'd practice more kicking tomorrow.

The next thing I knew, someone was shaking my shoulder, and I was trying to give them a kick.

"Josh, wake up. You're having a bad dream."

Mom was sitting on the side of my bed. "I'm sorry to wake you before you have to get up, but you were yelling and thrashing around in your bed."

I rubbed my eyes. "I think I was practicing karate kicks in my sleep," I said.

"Well, you might as well get up now. We can have breakfast together."

I lay there for a few minutes, thinking about what had happened last night. I'd better tell my mom at breakfast. Even though I didn't want her to worry, she'd get really mad if I weren't honest. And speaking of honest, I hadn't told her about my trouble at school or my big decision. We were going to need a pretty long discussion.

Sometimes when we lived in Woodview, we'd go out to McDonald's on a special date—usually when Dad worked late. Now that we were always alone together, we hadn't done that. I'd suggest it for tonight. Then I'd tell her everything.

My body felt stiff and achy when I crawled out of bed. I felt muscles I didn't know I had. Maybe a hot shower would loosen me up.

As the hot water splashed over my body, I relived my triumph of the night before. I, Joshua McIntire, had single-handedly—or single-footedly—fought off the enemies of darkness.

Well, maybe that was a little dramatic. I, Joshua McIntire, had managed to keep my cool and scare off those jerks. I jumped out of the shower feeling better already.

"Mom, how about if I take you out to McDonald's for dinner tonight?" I suggested at breakfast. "It's payday for me."

"Why, Joshua, I'd be honored," she said. "What's the occasion?"

"I've got some things to talk to you about," I replied.

"What?" she asked uneasily.

"Not now," I said. "That's why we're going out tonight."

"You're not in trouble, are you?" she asked. "Your father always used to take me to dinner if he'd done something he knew I'd be mad about."

I got a funny feeling in my stomach. Maybe all the dumb stuff I did was my dad's fault.

"Well, I've got some bad news and some good news," I said. "But you have to wait."

"Joshua, that's not fair. You get my curiosity aroused and then leave me hanging," she complained.

"Why don't you pick me up at Sonny's shop after work?" I suggested.

"I'll be there," she said. "Now I'm off to work. Have a good day."

She was out the door.

I pushed the toast crumbs into little piles on the table. Then I spelled out D-A-D. It reminded me of kindergarten when we'd spelled out words with rice. Back then I'd always spelled out M-O-M. I wondered if God was going to be able to do anything about getting my parents back together again.

I glanced up at the clock. I needed to hustle. I could hardly wait to tell Wendell about last night. I'd just loaded up my backpack when the doorbell rang.

"Hi, Josh. What's happenin'?"

"Well, outside of the fact that I have four more days of picking up trash on the playground, it's going good," I replied. "But here's the exciting news."

I told Wendell what had happened last night, and his eyes got big.

"Wow," he said, "that karate stuff really works. Weren't you scared?"

I hesitated. Should I tell him the truth?

"I was terrified," I said. "But somehow I remembered what I was supposed to do, and it worked. Those guys turned out to be real wimps."

"So, how are you doing with Samantha?" Wendell wanted to know.

"Okay, I guess," I answered. "At least she's stopped bossing me around all the time." Actually, I couldn't figure that scene out. All of a sudden Samantha had turned nice, and I didn't know if she was acting different or I was. Yesterday she had said, "That was a pretty dumb name for the group. I just picked it to bug you."

"I'm sorry I hit you," I had apologized. "I shouldn't have done that."

"I shouldn't have grabbed your backpack, either. I really started the whole thing."

She had stuck out her hand to shake. Shaking a girl's hand made me feel funny, but I did it anyhow, and Mrs. Bannister had walked up, smiling. "I'm glad to see you two have signed a truce," she had said. "Maybe now your group can get something accomplished."

I'd been so wrapped up in my own problems, I hadn't noticed Wendell's new shirt.

"Hey, I like your T-shirt," I said. "The Bears are great, aren't they?"

"Well, Brent Hillman is. I know that," said Wendell.

"Ditto," I said. We shuffled along in silence.

I was wondering how to tell Wendell about my becoming a Christian. But first I had to figure out how to tell my mom. Maybe Sonny would have some ideas.

Mrs. Bannister was drawing circles and lines all over the blackboard when we walked into class. In the middle of the maze, she'd written the word cooperation.

Oh, no, I thought. Not more cooperation.

"I want you to think about what cooperation means," she said. "Some of our groups have had some problems lately."

I was sure she glanced over in my direction when she said that.

"I want each group to think of four things that cooperation means. Then we're going to write them up on the board. You have fifteen minutes."

Ben, Maria, and I all looked at Samantha. We'd gotten used to her having both the first and last words. But she was quiet.

"I think cooperation means letting everybody

have their turn," I suggested. "Why don't you write that down, Maria?"

Samantha gave a little frown, but she didn't say anything.

"Well, I think cooperation is coming up with the best idea," she said.

I was about to criticize her suggestion, but I bit my tongue. Maria wrote it down below mine.

"What do you think, Ben?" Samantha asked.

I stared at her in surprise. I'd never heard her ask anybody else what they thought. She usually just told you what you thought.

"I haven't thought of anything," he said. "Come back to me."

It was Maria's turn. "I think cooperation is helping somebody out when they're in trouble," she said. "And I think we should help Josh out."

I'd never heard her utter more than three words at one time. And now she was talking about helping me out.

"That's a great idea," Samantha chimed in.

Now I really couldn't believe my ears. Samantha Sullivan was offering to help me out?

"Since we're Joshua's group, we could all help him pick up trash during recess. We'd be cooperating," Samantha continued.

She sounded a little bossy again, but I didn't mind. It was for a good cause.

"Mrs. Bannister, we've come up with the best definition of cooperation," she shouted across the room. Mrs. Bannister glanced our way in surprise. I'm not sure she really believed that our group could cooperate on anything.

Samantha started to explain in an authoritative voice, but Ben interrupted her. "Why don't you let Maria tell, Samantha? It was her idea."

Samantha looked ready to protest, but thought better of it.

In her soft, accented voice, Maria told Mrs. Bannister what we were going to do.

"That's a wonderful idea, Maria," she said. "But you'd better clear it with Mrs. Raymond. She might not approve of Josh getting help with his clean-up project."

"Can we ask right now?" asked Samantha. She was eager to move into action.

"I suppose so," said Mrs. Bannister. "But come right back. We're ready for our discussion."

Mrs. Raymond was in the hallway talking to the custodian. When she saw us coming, she waved.

"We're here to see you," announced Samantha.

Ben gave her a dirty look. "Maria has something she wants to ask about," said Ben.

Once more Maria explained her proposal.

Mrs. Raymond looked astonished. "Now, let me get this straight," she said. "You all want to help Josh serve his punishment for hitting Samantha? This is remarkable."

We all nodded.

"Even you, Samantha?" she asked.

Samantha nodded again.

"I think Mrs. Bannister must be doing a terrific job of teaching you what cooperation means," Mrs. Raymond said. She looked thoughtful for a moment. "Well, since Josh has four days left to work, and there are now four of you to do the job, his punishment will be taken care of after today."

I couldn't contain myself. I let out a whoop.

"Now, if Josh continues to disturb others in the hall, he might have another consequence," she said with a smile. "Hurry back to class."

The ongoing saga of Josh McIntire in Grandville might have a happy ending after all, I thought.

After school I walked over to the leather shop. It was filled with more customers than I'd ever seen there.

I hung up my jacket and started sweeping. By the time Sonny had helped all of the customers, I was almost done straightening the stacks of leather.

"How ya doin,' pardner?" Sonny asked.

I didn't know where to begin. But I told him all about my adventure of the night before and what had happened at school today.

"Praise the Lord," he said. "I knew you could do it—with a little help."

"My biggest problem right now," I said, "is telling my mom. I haven't even told her about running away from school."

"Well, that shouldn't be too hard," Sonny said. "At least you've got a happy ending. Let's rehearse what you're going to say."

I'd almost finished when Mom arrived to pick me up.

"Hi, Mr. Studebaker," she said.

"Please, call me Sonny," he reminded her. He stuck out his hand to clasp hers.

"I can't tell you how much I appreciate all you've done for Josh," she said.

"Well, he's a pretty special guy, as far as I'm concerned," he said.

I started to turn red.

"You guys have a great dinner together," he added.

Mom looked like she was going to say something but changed her mind. "Joshua's taking me out," she said.

"Not if I don't pay him," Sonny said. "I almost forgot." He reached into his old-fashioned cash register and took out a twenty.

"Isn't that too much?" I asked.

"Just a little bonus this week," Sonny answered.

"That's very kind of you, Mr. Stude—"

Sonny interrupted her. "Please, Mrs. McIntire. It's Sonny."

"Well, then you have to call me Charlotte," my mom answered.

This was getting ridiculous. We'd never get to dinner if they kept on talking about names.

"See you tomorrow, Josh. Have a good time," Sonny said.

My mom put her arm through mine, and we went out to the car. She was smiling in a dreamy sort of way. What was going on?

"So, where are we going to dinner, sir?" she asked in a laughing voice.

"Well," I said, waving my twenty-dollar bill, "I can afford just about any place."

"How about a Big Mac and fries?" she asked.

"I can even afford a chocolate shake and an apple pie," I replied.

McDonald's was crowded with families, and we got in one of the long lines. I saw some kids from class and waved. We ordered our food. I'd never paid for anything with a twenty-dollar bill before. Even the clerk looked impressed.

I led the way to a booth in the far corner.

"Well, Joshua, what's this big secret you have to tell me?" Mom asked the minute we sat down.

"Just give me a chance to eat," I said. "Then we can talk."

I tore into my Big Mac like I hadn't seen food for weeks. Working at Studebaker's always made me hungry. The fries were hot and crispy, just the way I liked them.

Mom wasn't eating. She was just watching me.

"What's the matter?" I asked.

"You are really growing up," she said. "You're even buying dinner for me. This is special."

My chest must have puffed out six inches. I hoped that she would still feel that way after I told her all about Samantha and running away from school. We finished our Big Macs, and I was polishing off an apple pie when Mom spoke again.

"Now what's the big news? I can't wait any longer."

I told her all about everything just like I'd rehearsed it with Sonny. Samantha, the fight, running away, my decision about Jesus, fighting off Pimples, and the meaning of cooperation.

She had tears in her eyes when I finished. I put my hand on hers across the table. "I'm sorry, Mom. I didn't mean to make you sad."

She dug around in her purse for a tissue and wiped her eyes.

"I don't know how I feel, Joshua," she said. "I want to spank you and hug you at the same time."

"I know," I said. "I messed up pretty bad, didn't I? I should have told you about all this sooner."

"I guess I understand, Joshua. But how can I trust you if you don't tell me what's going on?"

"I didn't want to get you all worried," I said. "And besides, I had Sonny to talk to."

She smiled. "He's a pretty special guy, isn't he?"

"Yeah," I said. "I don't know what I would have done without him."

"I'm pretty upset at Mrs. Raymond for not calling me when you ran away," she said.

"I think Sonny convinced her that you didn't need anything else to worry about," I explained.

"I don't ever want to hear you say that again, young man," she replied angrily. "You are the most important thing in my life, and I want to know about everything that happens to you—bad and good. Then we'll work it out together. And we can include both God and Sonny in that if you want to."

This conversation was going even better than I'd hoped.

"Now, Joshua, it's time to head for home. If you're going to earn your black belt in karate, you need plenty of rest."

We threw out our trash and headed for the car arm in arm.